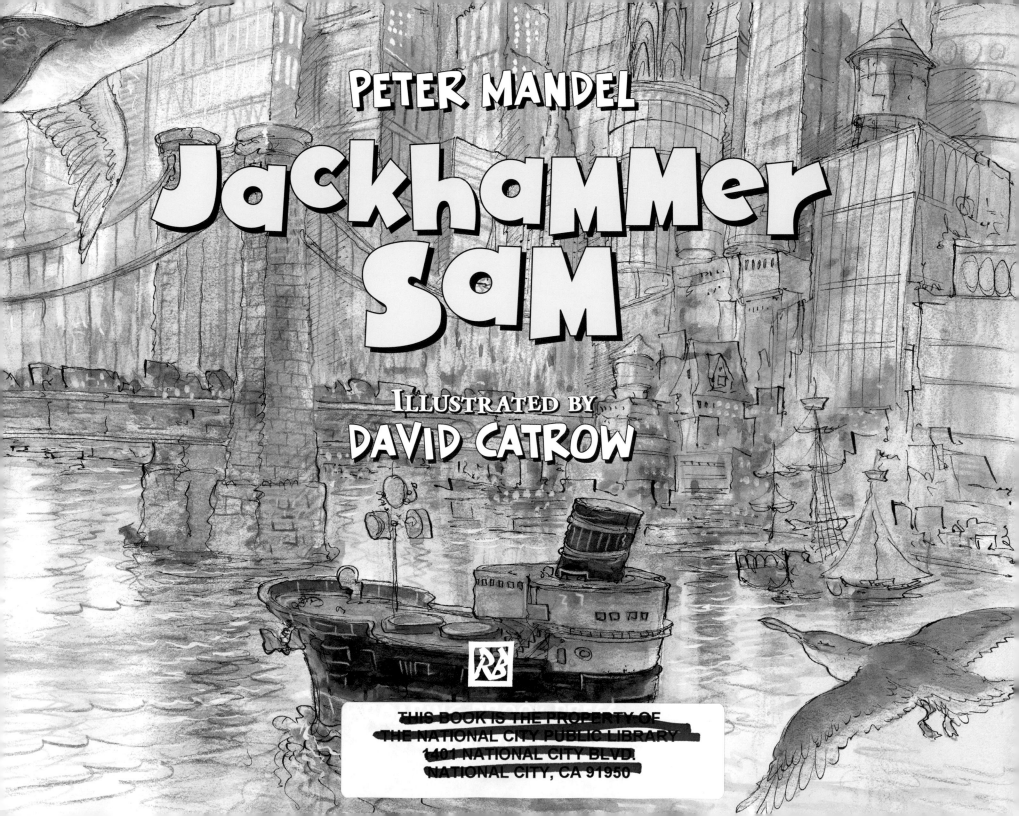

PETER MANDEL
Jackhammer Sam

ILLUSTRATED BY
DAVID CATROW

IN MEMORY OF MOM AND MARIAN, WHO
LOVED NEW YORK SO MUCH
— P.M.

TO MOM, FOR PUTTING UP WITH ALL MY RACKET
— D.C.

Text copyright © 2011 by Peter Mandel
Illustrations copyright © 2011 by David Catrow
Published by Roaring Brook Press
Roaring Brook Press is a division of Holtzbrinck Publishing Holdings Limited Partnership
175 Fifth Avenue, New York, New York 10010
mackids.com

Library of Congress Cataloging-in-Publication Data
Mandel, Peter, 1957–
    Jackhammer Sam / Peter Mandel ; illustrated by David Catrow.— 1st ed.
      p.   cm.
    Summary: A jackhammer operator boasts about his loud, sidewalk-blasting
skills.
    ISBN 978-1-59643-034-1
    [1. Stories in rhyme.   2. Jackhammers—Fiction.]   I. Catrow, David, ill.
II. Title.
PZ8.3.M347Jac 2011
[E]—dc22
                                          2010036341

Roaring Brook Press books are available for special promotions and premiums.
For details contact: Director of Special Markets, Holtzbrinck Publishers.

First Edition 2011
Book design by Andrew Arnold
Printed in August 2011 in China by South China Printing Co. Ltd., Dongguan City, Guangdong Province

10 9 8 7 6 5 4 3 2 1

Th' name's Jackhammer Sam.
Yeah, *that's* the man I am.

You may try to cross the street,
But there's a crack b'neath your feet.
'Cause I choppa-chop-concrete.
(An' I do not chop it neat.)

Yeah, my hammer sounds so sweet
When I chop it to a beat . . .

That I gotta make a song.
ATTA-RATTA-BINGA-BONG.

It might be loud. It could be long.
ATTA-RATTA-PINGA-PONG.

But I *never* hit it wrong.
ATTA-RATTA-DINGA-DONG.

See, there's a secret to my style.
When I work I take a while.

All the cars go single file.
An' I make policemen smile . . .

'Cause I build a monster pile
An' I drill a *city* mile.

I use my belly on the job.
It shakes like jelly (or a blob).

I dig so deep I just can't stop.
I mop the sewers
SLIP-SLAP-*SLOP.*

I pop th' steam pipes
RRRIP-DRIP-*DROP.*

I stop the subways
KREEK-KER-*PLOP.*

I once struck oil down below:
A mighty geyser, don'tcha know!

Plug your ears, she's gonna *blow!*
A river rushing. Watch 'er flow.

I turned a stop sign into "Go"
An' cut an oar so I could row.

My hammer drilled a giant's tooth.
My hammer paved the Rockies smooth.

My hammer broke th' break of day.
My hammer *drained* the Milky Way.

My hammer sings it loud 'n' strong.
An' I want *you* to sing along . . .

ATTA-**RATTA**-ᴘɪɴɢᴀ-ᴘᴏɴɢ.

ATTA-**RATTA**-ᴅɪɴɢᴀ-ᴅᴏɴɢ.

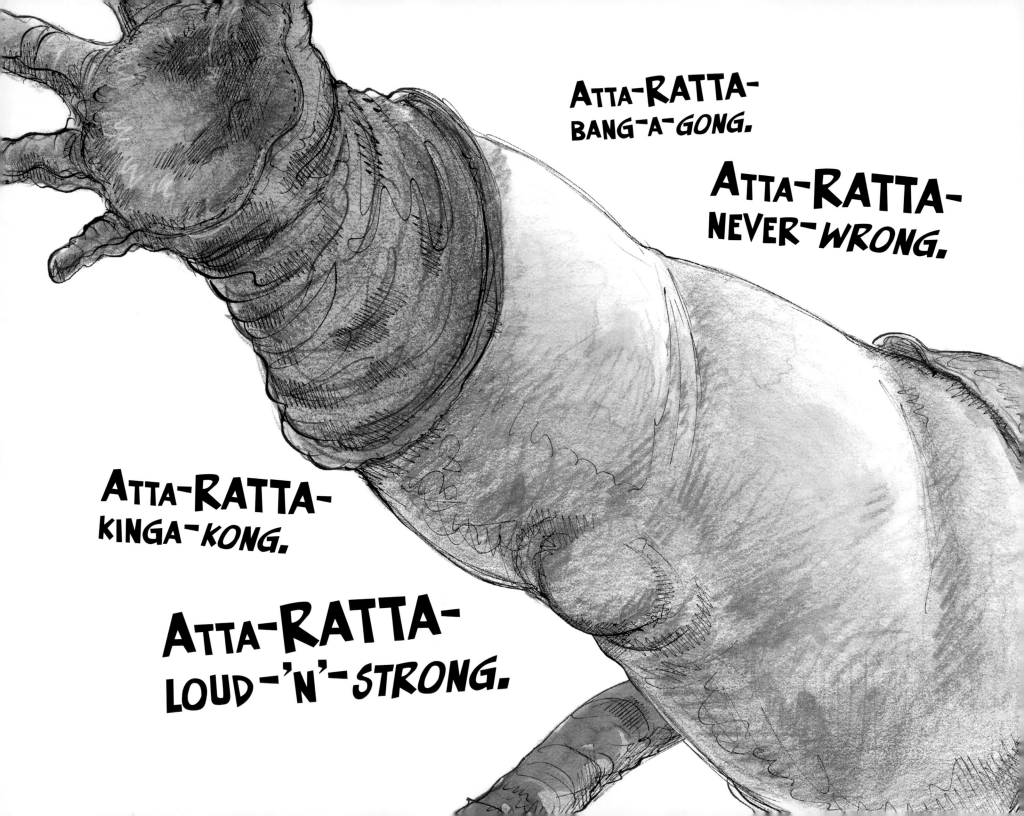

Th' name is Jackhammer Sam,
and that's my song.